The Christmas Fairy

Text by Maureen Spurgeon
Illustrated by Stephen Holmes

Brown Watson

ENGLAND

TWO men were talking outside in the street. Dolly could hear them quite clearly from the window sill where she sat.

"Quite a nip in the air," said one.

"Sure sign of Christmas on the way," said the other. "We always look forward to Christmas in our house!"

Dolly shivered, wishing she could pull her thin dress closer around her. If only she were still at the big house, she thought! Christmas had always been special, there...

That was when Dolly had lived in a big dolls' house, with the most delicious, warm smells wafting up from the downstairs kitchen and decorations in every room!

Once, there had even been a
Christmas tree in the big nursery,
with a fairy doll at the very top,
smiling down at them all. Dolly
thought she was beautiful.

"If only," she thought, "if only I could wear a lovely dress like that, and hold a wand in my hand... What wishes I'd give everyone for Christmas!"

Years passed, and the little girl who owned Dolly grew up. But, somehow, Dolly was always there at Christmas. Young visitors who called often played with her.

Dolly loved every minute – until, one Christmas, she got quite a shock. "Look, Mummy!" called out one little girl. "Look at this funny, old doll!"

"It was my mother's when she was about your age," smiled her aunty. "Then she gave her to me. When I have a little girl, I expect I'll pass it on to her, too!"

There had been many little girls over the years, Dolly remembered. They all grew up – but she stayed the same. And Christmas was still her favourite time of the year.

Then, one Christmas, something
happened. Underneath the big
Christmas tree, there was a big
parcel tied with ribbon. The little
girl could hardly wait to open it!

Inside was quite the most splendid doll, with soft curly hair, big blue eyes which opened and closed, and the loveliest dress Dolly had ever seen.

"I shall call her Arabella!" cried the little girl in delight. "Look, Mummy and Daddy! She can walk, too!"
Dolly could not help feeling sad.

The little girl played with Arabella
every day after that.
By the end of the Christmas
holidays, Dolly knew she had
been forgotten.

"What are you going to do with that old wooden doll, dear?" the little girl's Daddy asked his wife. "Is there anyone we know who would like it?"

"Not really," answered the little girl's Mummy. "Besides, children don't play with wooden dolls nowadays. She can go on the window sill for now."

And except for the times when the windows were cleaned or the window sill dusted, Dolly was quite alone. As Christmas drew near, she felt so cold, so miserable.

"Nobody would miss me here," she thought, looking out into the street. It was terrible, hearing the two men sounding so cheerful when she had never been so unhappy.

Suddenly, the door opened and the
little girl's mother hurried across the
room to open the window.
"Are you collecting rubbish?" she
called to the two men.

"Can you take a pile of old newspapers?"
"Be right with you, ma'am!" one shouted back. They didn't see Dolly falling out into the street!

She lay there for what seemed a very long time, cold and wet and wishing she could cry for help. Every so often, she would hear somebody talking about Christmas.

"Hello!" cried a voice, and Dolly
felt a rough hand picking her up.
"What have we got here?"
"Something for the rubbish tip, I
reckon, Mike!" said someone else.

Fear made Dolly feel colder than ever. Then the first man said, "Oh, I might as well take her home. Maybe my little girl will like her." Dolly did hope so!

"Well," said the man when he
showed Dolly to his daughter.
"What do you think?"
"Why can't she move her arms
and legs?" asked the little girl.

"Because she's made of wood, silly!" laughed the little girl's mother. "Your Nana had one just like this when I was about your age. She was fun to play with!"

"And," her mummy went on, "she's just what we need for Christmas!" Soon, the little girl was wiping all the mud and dirt off Dolly. And, as for her mummy...

She made Dolly the prettiest fairy
dress with silver wings, a tinsel
crown and a lovely, silver wand,
ready to grant all the wishes made
around the Christmas tree!